In a Minute, Mama Bear

Rachel Bright

Farrar Straus Giroux

New York

Mama Bear is in a hurry—
So *many* things to do today.

But Bella Bear cannot be rushed.
Bella Bear just wants to play!

"Arms up, *quick!*" says Mama Bear.
"Pajamas off! Let's get you dressed!"
"But I don't *want* to wear the blue!"
A certain Bella Bear protests.

"Blue's your favorite!" Mama sighs.
"*Come on*, Bella, what d'you say?"

"No!" says little Bella Bear.
"I want to wear the *red* today!"

It's time to go
downstairs for
breakfast.
Bella Bear is
counting *slow*.

"One...

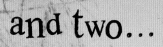and two...

and three...

and four..."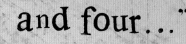

"**FIVE SIX!**"
Cries Mama. "Time to go!"

"I'm hungry!" Bella Bear proclaims.
"Oatmeal, eggs, and pancakes, please!"

"I've packed a picnic for the car,"
Says Mama, searching for her keys.

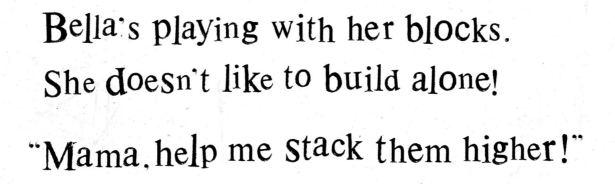

Bella's playing with her blocks.
She doesn't like to build alone!

"Mama, help me stack them higher!"

"Later, when we're back at home!"

"Come and brush your teeth, my love."
But brushing isn't Bella's thing.
Instead she's packing up her bag,
Deciding what she Ought to bring.

"In a minute, Mama Bear!
Play with me! Let's have some fun!"
"*Later*, Bella, not right now.
We're in a rush—we *have* to run!"

"Do you need to use the potty?
Quickly! Try—it's just here. See."

"I...think...I...*might*,"
says Bella Bear,
While browsing through
a book (or three).

"Time to put your coat on, Bella—
Shall I button it for you?"

"I'm big now!" Bella Bear insists.
"*I* can do my buttons too!"

Bella climbs into the car.
Mama buckles Bella up.
Now they're driving
off—*hooray!*

Then Bella shouts,
"*MY SIPPY CUP!*"

So *back* they go to get the cup.
Then AT LAST they're on their way!
To dance class... then the groceries...
Dry cleaning... then what *else* today?

But ALL the lights are turning RED.
Mama's face is red as well!
They'll be late for dance class now.
Mama starts to beep and YELL.

Then Mama glances back at Bella,
Sees her little worried face.
Suddenly she takes a breath...
This doesn't **have** to be a race.

Mama has a change of heart.
She wants to go a different way.
"New plan for us, my Bella Bear..."

"We're going to the park today!"

Bella Bear is SO excited—
No classes, errands, rush, or fuss.
"Slides and swings and snacks," says Mama.
"ALL day—just the two of us!"

At the park they run and jump,
They spin and whoosh and see and saw.
In the pond they splosh and Splash.
And feel the grass beneath each paw.

Together, they spot
shapes in clouds.
Mama's in a happy
mood.

They play for hours
without a care—
Till Bella's tummy
asks for food!

"Come on, Mama! Let's go home!"
And Mama says, "We really *should*...
But in a *minute*, Bella Bear.
This day has been so *very* good."

Mama Bear is moving *slowly*.
"One more seesaw, Bella Bear?"
"*Come on*, Mama Bear, I'm hungry!"
Bella gives her RIGHT NOW stare.

So, back home, they eat some supper,
Have a bath, and go to bed.

Mama lies beside her Bella,
Reads a book, and strokes her head.

The phone downstairs begins to ring.
Who can it be? It's very late.

"Aren't you going to get it, Mama?"
"In a minute..."

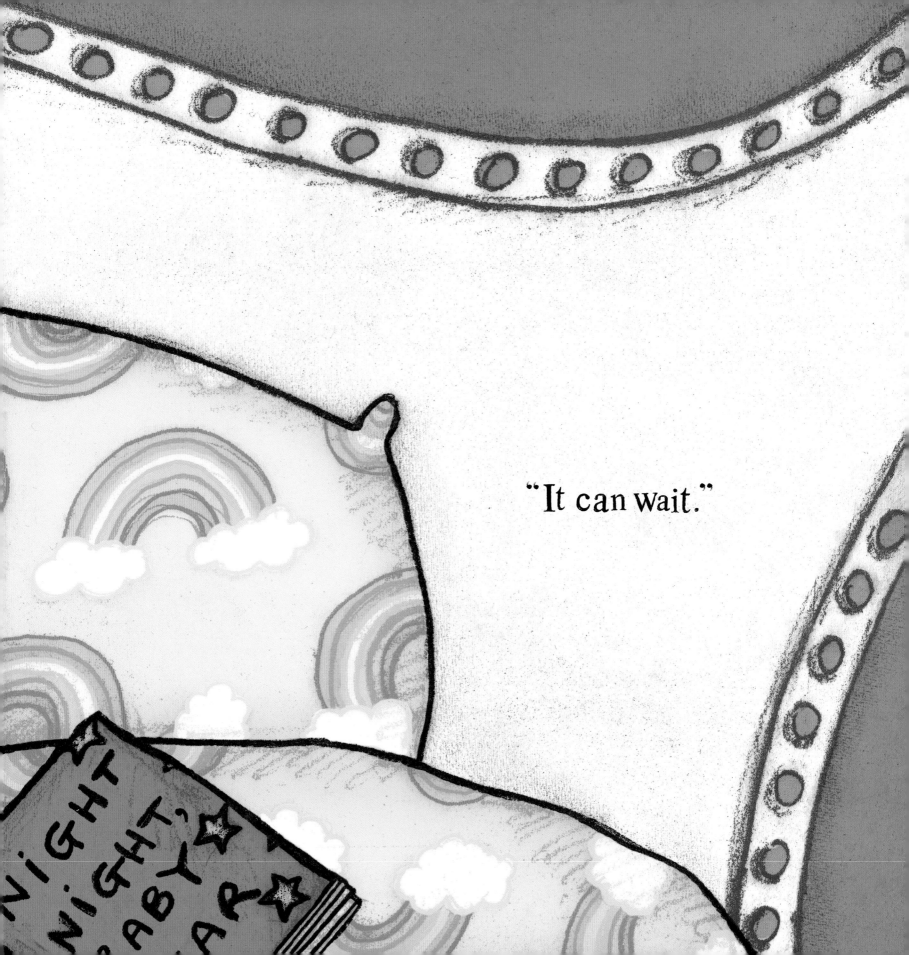

"It can wait."

For my darling River, who cannot be rushed . . . and
quite rightly so! You make every minute more fun.

Farrar Straus Giroux Books for Young Readers
An imprint of Macmillan Publishing Group, LLC
175 Fifth Avenue, New York, NY 10010

Copyright © 2019 by Rachel Bright
Color separations by Bright Arts (H.K.) Ltd.
Printed in China by RR Donnelley Asia Printing Solutions Ltd.,
Dongguan City, Guangdong Province
Designed by Monique Sterling
First edition, 2019
1 3 5 7 9 10 8 6 4 2

mackids.com

Library of Congress Cataloging-in-Publication Data

Names: Bright, Rachel, author, illustrator.
Title: In a minute, Mama Bear / Rachel Bright.
Description: First edition. | New York : Farrar Straus Giroux, 2019 |
    Summary: Mama Bear tries to hustle her cub through the day's activities
    and errands, but Bella Bear insists on going her own pace and showing Mama
    the value in taking her time.
Identifiers: LCCN 2018017985 | ISBN 9780374305789 (hardcover)
Subjects: | CYAC: Stories in rhyme. | Time management—Fiction. | Mothers and
    daughters—Fiction. | Bears—Fiction.
Classification: LCC PZ8.3.B7678 In 2019 | DDC [E]—dc23
LC record available at https://lccn.loc.gov/2018017985

Our books may be purchased in bulk for promotional, educational, or business use.
Please contact your local bookseller or the Macmillan Corporate and Premium Sales Department
at (800) 221-7945 ext. 5442 or by email at MacmillanSpecialMarkets@macmillan.com.